DARWIN
and the
GREAT
BEASTS

by KIN PLATT

Greenwillow Books

New York

Library of Congress Cataloging-in-Publication Data
Platt, Kin.
Darwin and the great beasts / by Kin Platt.
p. cm.
Summary: During a visit to the La Brea Tar Pit,
a boy named Darwin imagines what it would be
like to live in prehistoric times and try to outwit
the dinosaurs, saber-tooth tigers, and other huge beasts.
ISBN 0-688-10030-9
[1. Dinosaurs — Fiction.
2. Prehistoric animals — Fiction.
3. La Brea Pit (Calif.) — Fiction.
4. Imagination — Fiction.]   I. Title.
PZ7.P7125Dar 1992
[E] — dc20   90-39674   CIP   AC

To SCH,
for the beginning,
the middle,
and maybe the end

Author's Note

There are no dinosaurs or other creatures of the Great Reptile age to be found in or around the museum near the La Brea Tar Pit. I put them in to make the story more interesting.

Also, in case you haven't noticed, dinosaurs don't talk. Neither do mammoths or saber-tooth cats or wolves. They didn't read books, either. Books came much later.

CONTENTS

1. THE BEASTS IN THE TAR PIT

Darwin looked down at the tar pit. It was a small, dark lake. The water was quiet, but here and there he saw bubbles.

"That's the tar in the water, children," the teacher said. "There is oil underneath. The gas rises and makes the tar bed bubble."

The teacher's name was Miss Tell. She was

taking her class on a field trip to the La Brea Tar Pit and the science museum behind. They were looking around at huge, strange beasts they had never seen before.

Darwin saw an animal that looked like an elephant. But its tusks were much longer. They curved around almost in a circle. It was in the tarry water up to its knees.

Then he saw the little elephant next to it. It had hardly any tusks. But it looked stuck in the water, just like its mother.

"Those elephants are stuck," Darwin cried. "Why doesn't somebody help them get out of there?"

The other children looked at Darwin. They wanted to say they thought the same thing. They looked at Miss Tell.

"Those are mammoths, Darwin, not elephants," Miss Tell said. "They came long before elephants. Oh, over a million years ago. Their tusks were longer. They were much bigger, too."

Darwin decided now that these animals were dead. He knew elephants were supposed to live a long time. But a million years was too long. Even for a mammoth.

"How come they're stuck there?" he asked.

"They came down to the water to drink," Miss Tell said. "But their feet got stuck in the tar. Their bones were found there. Somebody made those statues of them to show us what they looked like. There's a saber-toothed cat over there. He was stuck here, too, and drowned."

Darwin didn't like the looks of the giant saber-tooth. Its long teeth curved down below its chin. He was glad no saber-tooths were living in this neighborhood now.

"When an animal got stuck in the tar," Miss Tell said, "other animals jumped in to attack it. Then they got stuck in the tar, too. That's what happened to that saber-tooth."

"I'm glad," Darwin said. "That mean saber-tooth never got near the mama mammoth and her baby."

"All kinds of animals got stuck here," Miss Tell said. "There were great big wolves, then. They were called dire wolves. More of them were trapped here than any other animal. Birds flew in, too, got their feet stuck, and couldn't fly out. This tar pit has been here for thousands of years."

"How come it's so sticky?" Darwin asked. "That mammoth looks big and strong enough to get out of anything, if it wanted to."

"Tar is sticky stuff," Miss Tell said. "It's formed by the gas underneath. We use tar to cover roofs and to make roads or seal seams on ships. Tar is also called pitch and asphalt."

"Is it like quicksand?" Darwin asked.

"Not exactly, but just as bad," Miss Tell said. "The more the stuck creatures tried to escape, the stickier they got, and the deeper they sank. Now let's go inside. You'll see the great creatures that lived here long ago. You'll see a movie about the biggest of them all, the giant dinosaurs."

Darwin looked back at the stuck mammoths. "I bet I could have saved them," he said to himself.

2. DARWIN AND THE MAMMOTH

The big mammoth looked back at Darwin. "What?" she said.

"Don't move," Darwin said. "Don't try so hard to get out. It only gets worse."

"You're telling me," the mammoth said. "What *is* this stuff?"

"It's tar," Darwin said. "It's sticky stuff. The

more you struggle, the more stuck you get. Everybody gets stuck and drowns here."

"Well, why don't they put up a sign or something?" the mammoth said. "I just stepped in for a drink of water."

"Don't feel bad," Darwin said. "It fools everybody. I'll get help. Stay right here."

"Well, hurry it up. There's a big saber-tooth over there. Did you ever see such teeth? If I wasn't stuck in here, I'd throw him from here to there."

Darwin ran to get help. He ran through a thick forest. The trees hid him from mean-looking creatures. He ran through high grass. He saw birds with enormous wings. The grass hid Darwin from the birds.

"Help!" Darwin cried. "A mammoth is stuck in the tar with her baby!"

He tripped over a tree root. His toe hurt. He

wasn't wearing shoes. He wasn't wearing much of anything. That's how everybody went around in those days long ago.

He saw a big mammoth eating. "Come quickly," Darwin cried. "We've got a couple of mammoths stuck in the tar pit."

"Sorry," the mammoth said. "This is my lunch hour. I still have two or three trees to go before I'm full." He kept stuffing his mouth with leaves and grass.

"But this is an emergency," Darwin said.

"So is this," the mammoth said. "I haven't eaten for two days."

Darwin ran on. He found a bunch of mammoths together. "Help!" Darwin cried. "There's a mammoth in the tar pit with her baby. They're stuck and going to drown there."

"That must be Mildred," one of them said. "She's such a dope. Anybody with any sense can smell tar. I feel sorry for little Debbie having such a dumb mother."

"But we can save them," Darwin said. "We can pull them out."

"Out of the tar pit?" a mammoth said. "Are you kidding?"

"I figured out how to do it. Come on!" Darwin cried.

The mammoths followed Darwin. "We're all Mildred's sisters," one told him. "We're Debbie's aunts. Last week we had to pull Mildred out of a briar patch. She's getting to be a pain."

They came to the tar pit. "Now what?" one mammoth said. "You're not getting us in there. We're not that stupid."

"Pull down that tree," Darwin said. "That will reach."

They pulled the tree down. "Now what?" they asked.

Darwin ran out on the tree. He pulled off some thin branches. He made a rope. He tied one end to the tree and the other to Debbie's tail. He made a thicker rope and tied it to Mildred's tail and the tree.

"Now pull hard on the tree," Darwin said.

The mammoths pulled hard. Debbie and Mildred came unstuck. Mildred flapped her ears. "Whew! What a relief. I thought that was the end."

"Mildred," one of her sisters said, "you're such a dope. Can't you smell tar? Mama always told us not to drink there."

"I've got a cold in my nose," Mildred said. "I can't smell anything today."

Darwin waved good-bye. The saber-tooth gave him a dirty look. "Why don't you mind your own business?" he told Darwin.

3. THE HUNTERS AND THE HUNTED GIANTS

Miss Tell led her class into the large museum hall. "Here is the dinosaur world," she said. "They first lived about two hundred million years ago, and they ruled for more than one hundred million years. They were the greatest creatures on the planet. Then suddenly they disappeared. Nobody knows why."

Darwin looked up. He looked up and up and up. He couldn't believe this thing. The sign said:

Brontosaurus
THE GREAT SAUROPOD
ONE OF THE LARGEST LAND CREATURES

Darwin had seen pictures of dinosaurs before. But now he was standing close to one. It was higher than a building. It looked longer than a city block. It was a skeleton, of course. All those giant bones were put together to show how the huge creature looked in real life. The long neck seemed to stretch out forever. So did the tail.

Darwin had to imagine how it would look with its flesh and skin on. "Boy, I sure would like to ride on one of these," he said to himself. "Way up there on top."

"What's a sauropod?" Darwin asked.

"Sauropod means lizard-footed," Miss Tell said. "And dinosaur means terrible lizard. Scientists used to think that all dinosaurs were a kind of giant lizard or reptile. But a lot of new discoveries are being made about dinosaurs these days. While lizards are cold-blooded, dinosaurs probably were different. Some scientists now think they were warm-blooded, just like mammals and birds."

"How much did this one weigh?" a girl asked. Her name was Amy.

"About thirty tons," Miss Tell said.

I would have guessed nearly a hundred, Darwin thought.

"But there was another one," Miss Tell said. "It was a little smaller but much heavier. That one was called *Brachiosaurus*. It probably weighed eighty tons."

"I wouldn't want one of those stepping on my

feet," Darwin said to himself.

Darwin remembered that elephants ate a lot. They were very big and had to keep up their energy. This dinosaur was much bigger. "I bet they had to eat a lot," he said.

"Yes," Miss Tell said. "But they were plant-eaters. You know, vegetarians. They were very peaceful. They didn't hunt other animals to eat them."

"Which ones did?" Amy asked.

Darwin looked at Amy. That was a good question, he thought.

Miss Tell pointed over their shoulders. "The theropods were the meat-eaters. That one is *Allosaurus*. It means different lizard. But the largest one of all was *Tyrannosaurus*. The tyrant king."

Darwin turned. He stared with the others. He saw a large creature standing on two hind legs. It had small front arms with large claws. Its head was bigger than he was. Its teeth were very long and curved. So were the thick claws on its feet. Its tail was long, too.

Amy closed her eyes. "I don't like that one," she said.

I don't like it, either, Darwin thought.

"How much did that one weigh?" Darwin asked.

"About six tons," Miss Tell said. "*Tyrannosaurus* was about fifty feet long and twenty feet high. But although it was smaller than *Brontosaurus*, it hunted it down. Its teeth were six inches long. It could kill anything."

"I knew I didn't like it," Darwin said to himself.

"Now let's look at the dire wolves and the big cats," Miss Tell said.

Darwin looked back at *Brontosaurus*. "I bet I could have saved it," he said to himself.

4. DARWIN HELPS A FRIEND

Darwin stepped out of his cave. He was holding his sling. He found some small stones. He put them into a bag tied around his waist. He had made the bag out of dried crocodile skin. The air was cold, and he shivered. He waved the sling. "If any of those mean-looking birds come at me today, I'll shoot them down."

He ran and jumped over rocks. He didn't see the deep hole in time. It nearly covered him. "Jeepers!" he said. "Those brontosaurs sure have big feet. I can take a bath in here."

He climbed out. He heard somebody cry, "Help!"

Darwin looked all around. He didn't see anybody.

"Up here," a voice said.

Darwin saw four thick trees.

"Those are my legs," the voice said. "Look higher."

Darwin looked up and up. He saw a long neck above the "tree stumps." The neck curved down, and he saw a head. Now he knew what it was. A brontosaur!

"Are you talking to me, Bronty?" he said. "What's wrong?"

"A tyrannosaur is after me. He's been chasing me all day. I'm pooped. I can't run another step," the brontosaur said.

Darwin looked. "I don't see one," he said.

"He's coming up over the hill back there," the beast said. "I can see him from way up here."

Darwin looked at the hill. A huge form came up. The beast was running on his two back legs. He was making mad sounds.

"I see him," Darwin said. "Don't worry. I'll take care of him for you."

"Mind if I ask how?" the brontosaur asked. "Your teeth are too small. You couldn't even crack a coconut."

Darwin held up his sling. "This sling works better than teeth. I'll knock him right out of the park."

"Well, you better get started," the huge creature said. "Here he comes. Those jaws can swallow a buffalo."

"He'll have to catch me first," Darwin said. He put one of his stones in his sling. It was made of a long strip of lizard skin. His father had made it for him.

The tyrannosaur came closer. His red eyes gleamed. "Fresh meat!" he roared. "I never ate one of you before."

Darwin swung his sling around faster and faster.

"Are you kidding with that thing?" The monster laughed.

Darwin threw the stone. It whizzed at the head of the tyrannosaur. "Bull's-eye," Darwin said.

The monster opened his huge jaws. He caught the stone in his teeth. He swallowed it. "I like nuts," he said.

Darwin slung another stone. Then another. *Tyrannosaurus* caught the stones in his mouth. He swallowed them in two more gulps. He came closer. Darwin ran. He stopped and slung another stone. The towering beast ate that one, too.

Darwin was near the cliff. He had to stop. He had one stone left. He threw it with all his might. The beast swallowed that one, too. He opened his jaws to swallow Darwin.

Suddenly he moaned. *"Ow!* I've got a tummy ache." He held his belly. He leaned over the cliff. He leaned too far.

Darwin saw him fall and crash far below. He returned to the brontosaur. "All clear," he said. "You can come out now."

The brontosaur looked at Darwin with wonder. "That was pretty good, kid. Are you new here in this neighborhood?"

5. GIANT WOLVES AND SABER-TOOTHED CATS

Darwin looked at the great wolf and the sign under it. DIRE WOLF, the sign said. *Canis dirus*. The wolf was gray. His head was very large. He had huge jaws and sharp teeth.

"Why is it called a dire wolf?" Darwin asked.

Miss Tell read from the La Brea museum booklet. "It was named that over a hundred years ago," she said, "because it was larger and different from wolves we see today. Five thousand years ago, these wolves were hunting here in La Brea. In fact, more dire wolves have been found in the tar pit than any other of the great meat-eating animals."

"He's got a bigger head and chest," Amy said. "Also his legs are shorter, I think."

Darwin nodded. "That's just what I was thinking," he said to himself. "She's pretty smart, that Amy."

"How come so many fell in?" Darwin asked. "Didn't they know they'd get stuck in the tar?"

"If they knew, they forgot," Miss Tell said. "When they saw another animal stuck, they jumped in to attack it. And even if they killed the other one, they got stuck, too."

"Why do they call this place the La Brea Tar Pit?" Amy asked.

Hey, no fair, Darwin thought. I was just going to ask that one myself.

"The word *brea* is Spanish for tar or pitch," Miss Tell said. "*La* Brea means *The* Pitch. Pitch, we know, is like tar. This is oil country. The oil comes up from the ground. It brings the tarry pitch up with it. Then the oil evaporates and leaves the tarry film all around the water surface."

"How many of those dopey dire wolves fell in?" Darwin asked. He was sure Amy would ask that, if he didn't hurry.

Miss Tell looked at the booklet. "1,646 dire wolf fossils were found. And 1,029 saber-tooths. That's the giant cat that lived around here. It was as big as a lion or tiger."

"I don't see any," Amy said.

"There's one right behind you," Miss Tell said.

Amy turned her head. She screamed. "Yipe!"

"It won't hurt you," Darwin said. "It's not real."

More children screamed when they saw the saber-tooth. It was crouching right there in the museum hall. It looked ready to pounce on somebody. Its jaws were wide open. The two long front teeth were curved like daggers. They were over six inches long. They came below the big cat's chin.

Darwin read the sign underneath it.

Smilodon fatalis
LATE DESCENDANT
OF THE *Megantereon* DIRKTOOTH

"What's a dirktooth?" Amy asked Miss Tell.

"A dirk is a small dagger or knife," Miss Tell said.

"I knew it," Darwin said to himself.

Amy clapped her hands. "Just like a saber is a small sword," she said.

Darwin looked at Miss Tell. She smiled at Amy.

"Exactly," Miss Tell said. "So you can imagine, boys and girls. With swords like that in their jaws, the saber-toothed cats were fearsome creatures."

But they were dumb, too, Darwin thought, if they fell in the tar pit.

"Now we'll see some of the other great creatures," Miss Tell said. The class followed her. Except for Darwin and Amy.

"I wasn't really afraid of it, Darwin," Amy said.

"I know," Darwin said. "You were just pretending. I bet I could figure out how to handle it."

Amy's eyes opened wide. "You could?" she said.

6. OUT OF THE CAVE INTO TROUBLE

There were caves under the hill. During the Ice Age, they were the warmest places to be. The people who lived in caves knew what they were doing. They ate and slept there. Rent was free. The supermarket was just outside. All you had to do was walk around and find what you liked to eat.

If you lived in a cave, you had a great view.

Unless there was something nasty-looking outside with big teeth looking in. Then maybe you wished you had a door.

Darwin came out of cave number four. Amy came out of cave number five. They were next-door cave neighbors.

Darwin had his sling over his shoulder. His pouch filled with stones was tied to his side.

Amy carried a long, thin pole and a bag of pebbles.

"You can't kill anything with that," Darwin said.

"Oh, no? Watch this," Amy said. She put a pebble in her mouth. She picked up the thin stick. She pointed it up and blew.

A bird flying overhead said, "Ow!" The bird fell down.

Amy picked it up and threw it back into her cave. "Well, there's dinner," she said.

Darwin looked at the pole. It was hollow inside. "Hey, that's neat," he said. "But what if you didn't have a pole you could blow through?"

Amy shrugged. "I'd invent something else."

They walked deep into the woods. They heard animals screaming. Birds were screeching. Lions were roaring.

"What's all that noise?" Amy asked.

"It's coming from the tar pit," Darwin said. "If you step in there, you get stuck. Everybody who jumps in to get you gets stuck, too. It's very gooey, sticky stuff."

Amy stopped and pointed. A mother deer was hiding with her fawn. "What's wrong?" Amy asked.

"Shh," the deer whispered. "There's a pack of dire wolves after us."

"How many are in a pack?" Darwin asked.

"A lot," the deer said. "They're mean. Be careful."

"They're pretty dumb, too," Darwin said. "I know how to handle them."

The pack of dire wolves trotted by. They were silent as ghosts. Darwin stepped out. The big wolves stopped.

"Did you hear what happened to that dumb saber-tooth?" he said to them.

"No. What?" one of them growled.

"He's stuck in the tar pit down there," Darwin said.

The wolves grinned. "Oh, boy, let's go," they said.

Amy looked at Darwin. "You told them a big fib."

"I know," Darwin said. "Now I have to tell another one."

They heard an awful snarling sound from behind a bush. A giant saber-tooth was about to spring at them. Darwin winked at Amy. "Wasn't that dumb of those dire wolves to get themselves stuck in the tar pit? They'll never get out."

"What's that?" the saber-tooth said.

Darwin pointed. "A whole pack of them. In the tar pit over there. Can't you hear them yelling?"

The saber-tooth listened. "Excuse me," he said. "I've got to check this out."

They watched the giant cat rush off. Amy shook her head. "Darwin," she said. "You're the world's biggest fibber."

The mama deer came up to them. "Don't blame him, young lady," she said. "He saved our lives. Come along, Matilda."

Darwin watched the deer walk away. He and Amy shook hands. "How come when I tell fibs, nobody believes me?" Amy said.

Darwin smiled. "Maybe you have to practice more."

7. DINOSAURS YOU DON'T WANT AT YOUR PARTY

"Now we see two different kinds of dinosaurs," Miss Tell said. "Those with armor. Those with horns."

The children crowded around the first one. The sign underneath said *Polacanthus.* It was about fifteen feet long. It looked as if nothing could hurt it. Along its back and down its long, thick tail were two rows of thick sawlike spikes of armor. Its bulky body was covered with armor plates. It had four thick legs. The back legs were higher. The front legs were short and curved.

"It looks like a tank," Darwin said.

"It looks like a lizard-crocodile-dragon," Amy said.

"It looks weird," somebody else said.

"It looks like a battleship," another said.

Next was a giant beast about twenty feet long. It had armor over its thick body and over its skull. Its tail looked like a thick, heavy club. The sign said *Ankylosaurus*.

"I kind of like this one," Amy said.

"How come?" Darwin asked.

"It has tiny teeth," Amy said.

"It was a vegetarian, not a meat-eater," Miss Tell said. "It needed soft plants to feed on."

Darwin walked ahead. He stared up at a huge beast with a large, curved horn on its nose. It looked like a rhinoceros but was much bigger. Its head was twice as big as Darwin was. The sign said *Monoclonius.*

"That horn could come in handy in a fight," Darwin said to himself.

Next to that was a dinosaur with two horns on its head and one on its nose. *Triceratops.* Another one had five horns. Two were on its head. One was on its nose. And two small ones were on its cheeks. The sign said *Pentaceratops.* The next one had a horn on its nose and spikes all around its head. This was *Styracosaurus.*

"What would you do if you met them?" Amy asked.

"I'd run," Darwin said.

"There's one more you haven't met," Miss Tell said.

Iguanodon, the sign said. The huge dinosaur towered above them. The children screamed.

"It has three-toed feet," Amy said.

"It has five-fingered hands," Darwin said.

"Yeah, but look at those thumbs," Amy said. "They look more like spikes than thumbs."

"Maybe it used them for a toothbrush," Darwin said.

"Look at those teeth," somebody said.

"Well, children," Miss Tell said, "what do you think?"

"Yech," they said.

Miss Tell looked up at the creature. "I have to admit, it's not exactly pretty. But it has small teeth. So we know it was a vegetarian. It didn't eat people."

"How big was it standing up?" Darwin asked.

Miss Tell looked inside the booklet. "It was fifteen feet tall and weighed five tons. It was twenty-five feet long. As you can see, it has very strong legs. It probably had to be able to run very fast to escape the meat-eating dinosaurs."

"I bet I could outrun that thing," Darwin said to himself. "Unless he was mad at me about something."

8. DANGER ON LAND AND SEA

Darwin and Amy came out of their caves. Darwin had his sling and stones to throw. Amy had her long, hollow blowstick.

They walked around the swamp. They climbed a hill. The ground started to shake. They stopped. They heard heavy clumping sounds.

Amy pointed. A huge, monstrous beast came closer. "What's that thing? It's bigger than a tank."

"Don't worry," Darwin said. "It only looks like a tank. I bet it's wearing fake armor."

The huge dinosaur glared at them. "You're wrong, kid. This is the new, improved stuff. It's waterproof and shrinkproof. If I knew what a bullet is, I'd say it's bulletproof, too. Trouble is, it weighs a ton."

Darwin whirled the stone in his sling. It made a whistling sound. He threw it hard. It made a funny noise when it landed.

Clunk!

"Ha, ha," the monster said. "That tickled."

"Huh?" Amy said. "It bounced off." She picked a pebble from her bag. She put the pebble in her mouth. She aimed her blowstick at the grinning monster. She blew hard.

It bounced off, too. *Plink.*

"That was a good shot, too," Amy said.

"So was mine," Darwin said.

The monster rumbled closer. His long tongue flicked out. He grinned and opened his huge jaws. "Hold it right there," he said. "I bet I can eat you both at the same time."

Amy looked at Darwin. "I think he means it," she said.

"Let's go swimming," Darwin said.

"Good idea," Amy said.

They ran down the hill to the water.

"Hey, no fair," the dinosaur said. "My feet hurt. I can't run that fast."

"Sorry about that," Darwin said.

"Have a nice day," Amy said.

They dived into the water and swam away.

They swam around until they got tired.

Darwin looked at the sun. "Time to go home,"

he said. "We don't want to run into any night monsters."

Amy looked around. "I don't see any," she said.

"Okay, let's go," Darwin said.

A huge head popped out of the water. "Hi, kids," it said. "Going my way?"

"Which way are you going?" Amy said.

"Which way are *you* going?" the creature said.

"The other way," Darwin said. They swam faster.

The sea creature laughed. "Wait! I'll give you a lift."

Its huge, scaly tail flicked out of the water. Amy and Darwin flew through the air. They landed on the shore.

"Thanks," Darwin said. "You had us worried."

"Are you a sea dragon?" Amy asked.

"I'm the *good* sea dragon," it said. "I think I'm the only one."

"That's good," Darwin said. "We'll look for you again."

"Better not," it said. "We all look the same."

"There goes swimming," Darwin said.

9. THE FLYING DRAGONS

"Oh, wow!" Darwin said. "Look at this."

Amy came over. "What is it? A giant bat or a vampire?"

Miss Tell read from the museum booklet. "It's the giant bird called the pterodactyl. It's a flying reptile. Pterodactyls ruled the skies millions of years ago."

The giant bird had twelve-foot wings. One of its fingers was six feet long. It had a long, toothless beak. On the back of its skull was a long, bony crest.

Its body was no larger than a turkey's!

"It wasn't a flapping bird," Miss Tell said. "It was a glider. Those enormous wings helped it glide around all day. All it needed was the smallest breeze. It would just stretch its wings and be lifted in the air like a piece of paper. It weighed only about twenty pounds."

"It looks like a dive bomber," Darwin said.

Miss Tell smiled. "Well, in a way it was. It was the greatest flying machine of its time. That crest on its skull was used like a rudder. It helped it change its direction in the air."

"Where did it come from?" Amy asked.

"All around here and down to Texas," Miss Tell said. "Just like the mammoths and wolves and lions. Because its wings were so large, it had to live on cliffs."

Darwin could see the huge bird spotting its prey. Then hurtling down like a silver bullet from the sky.

Miss Tell turned to another page. "It says here some were found in Texas with a wingspan of forty feet! That's the jumbo jet pterodactyl. They called the jumbo one *Pteranodon*."

"They must have needed a long run for take-off," Darwin said.

"That was their problem," Miss Tell said. "With those great wings, they couldn't run. They had to lift off straight up in the air when a breeze or air current came."

"Pigeons can fly straight up without a run," Darwin said. "I guess that's why they're still around."

"I'm glad," Amy said. "I'd rather feed a pigeon."

"Did any of these get stuck in the tar pit?" Darwin asked. He couldn't imagine that. With those great wings, they would be stuck here forever.

Miss Tell was shaking her head. "No," she said. "All the bones of birds and animals found in the tar pit are from the last forty thousand years. The pterodactyls were around millions of years earlier. Also, pterodactyls had large brains. They were too intelligent to be trapped in the tar."

"How about other birds?" Amy asked.

"Golden eagles, condors, and vultures have been found," Miss Tell said. "Do you know why it is called a pterodactyl?"

"Because it's hard to spell?" Amy guessed.

"Because it's hard to pronounce?" Darwin guessed.

"Not exactly," Miss Tell said. "Its long fourth finger had a wing growing on it. That's what *Pterodactylus* means—wing finger. Now let's all go see the movie. It's all about the great dinosaurs who once ruled the world."

"They weren't so tough," Darwin said. "I could have handled them."

Miss Tell looked at him. "Really, Darwin?"

"Well," Darwin said. "I think so." He looked at Amy.

Amy looked at Darwin and smiled. "I think so, too." She thought for a moment. "I think *we* could have."

10. CATCH ME IF YOU CAN

Darwin and Amy came out of their caves. It was early in the day, and the air was chilly. Darwin was wearing his cutoff bearskin shorts. Amy was wearing a bikini made of tiger skin. The ground was cold under their bare feet.

Amy shivered. "My toes are freezing. Why doesn't somebody invent shoes or something?"

Darwin pulled two large leaves from a plant. "Maybe these will help. Wrap them around your feet."

Amy tried that. "That feels good." She stood up. "How does it look?"

"Kind of weird," Darwin said. "Maybe you need a smaller size. Let's see if you can run in them."

Amy tried running. "Kind of floppy," she said. "But not bad. You ought to do it, too. It keeps your feet nice and warm, Darwin."

"I need bare feet for running," Darwin said. "Some of these dinosaurs are pretty fast. They take giant steps."

"Not me," a voice said. "I can't run at all."

They looked around. They couldn't see anything.

"Up here," a voice said.

They looked up and saw the sun. Then the

sun disappeared. They saw great wings instead. The wings were so large, they blotted out the sun.

"Tail flaps down," the voice said. "Prepare for landing."

There was a rush of wind. A giant bird swooped down. It picked Darwin up with its right foot. It picked Amy up in its left foot. Then it zoomed up in the air again.

"Flying is more fun," the bird said. "It beats walking. You don't freeze your feet. You don't step on sharp stones. And it's the best way to see the country."

"Are you a pterodactyl?" Amy asked.

The bird giggled. "I don't know what I am," it said. "Someone will probably think of a name for me later. How do you like the trip so far?"

"It's okay," Darwin said. "As long as you don't drop us."

"Don't you have parachutes for passengers?" Amy asked.

"Don't worry," the bird said. "Be happy."

The giant bird flew them over mountains and rivers and lakes. It flew them over swamps and forests. It glided in the sky without ever flapping its wings. It flew in wide, gentle circles.

"All we need is a little bit of breeze," the bird said. "The rest is easy as pie."

"What's pie?" Amy asked.

"Beats me," the bird said. "It's an expression I heard."

Amy pointed to a smoking mountain. "What's that?"

"It's smoking," the bird said. "It never did that before."

They flew over the thick smoke. Darwin saw fire beneath the smoke. "It's a volcano," he said. "Watch out!"

The smoke was making them cough. "That stuff is awful," the bird said. "It makes my eyes water. I can't breathe." The bird coughed some more. "I better take you home. I can't fly and cough at the same time."

It dropped them off near their caves. Darwin and Amy waved. "Thanks for the ride," they both said.

The bird coughed. "My pleasure," it said. It coughed again. "Somebody ought to do something about that mountain. That smoke is polluting the air. See ya." It flew off coughing.

Amy looked down at her feet. "Hey, my shoes fell off."

"That's okay," Darwin said. "*We* didn't."

11. SAYING GOOD-BYE TO A SABER-TOOTH

Everybody in the museum hall was finished looking at things. They were so used to the great creatures around them, they didn't jump or scream anymore.

"Well," Miss Tell said, "how did you like it?"

"It was neat," a girl said.

"It was great," a boy said.

"It was fun," Amy said.

Darwin looked at her. She was smiling. She looked as if she meant it. "You know what I liked best? It was that sea dragon."

Amy nodded. "The good sea dragon," she said.

Miss Tell looked at Amy and Darwin. She looked all around the museum hall. "Sea dragon? I don't see any sea dragon here."

"You don't really see them," Amy said, "until they pop up at you."

"But there's only one good one," Darwin said. "You have to be careful."

Miss Tell was smiling. "Whatever for?" she said.

"They all look the same," Amy said.

Miss Tell looked at them. She waved to the others. "Come along now, children. Our bus back to school is waiting."

The other children walked with her. Amy and Darwin followed them.

"It's too bad you missed the mammoths," Darwin said.

"Oh, you mean Debbie and Mildred?" Amy said.

Darwin stared. "How did you know?"

"I happened to be there, too," Amy said. "I was on the other side of the pit. You were so busy saving them, you never saw me."

Darwin shook his head. "I didn't see any-body."

"That's because I was hiding up in a tree," Amy said.

Darwin blinked. "What were you doing there?"

"A big saber-toothed cat chased me there," Amy said. "It took awhile before I got rid of him."

"How did you do that?" Darwin asked. He

remembered seeing a saber-tooth near the tar pit.

"He was coming awfully close," Amy said. "Jumping up, and I could feel his hot breath."

"Wow," Darwin said. "Weren't you scared?"

"Of course I was scared," Amy said. "I kept telling him to get lost, but he wouldn't listen. Then I told him he had bad breath and ought to do something about that."

"You did?" Darwin said, surprised. I bet I never would have thought of that, he thought to himself. "So what happened?"

Amy grinned. "He ran down to the tar pit to rinse his mouth out. Maybe he tried to gargle, too."

They were outside the museum now with Miss Tell and the other children. Miss Tell said, "You can all have another look at the tar pit lake, if you like."

The children ran all around to see the stuck animals.

Darwin looked at Amy. "The saber-tooth came here?"

"Well, sure," Amy said. "It looks like a lake full of water, doesn't it?" She pointed. "That's him, right there."

Darwin looked. He saw the giant saber-tooth stuck in the tar pit. He laughed. "So that's what happened to him," he said. "That was good thinking, Amy."

Amy nodded. "I thought so, too," she said.

Then they got on the bus and talked all the way back to school.

BOOKS BY KIN PLATT

For Young Readers

The Blue Man
Big Max
Sinbad and Me
The Boy Who Could Make Himself Disappear
Mystery of the Witch Who Wouldn't
Hey, Dummy
Chloris and the Creeps
Chloris and the Freaks
Chloris and the Weirdos
Mystery of the Missing Moose
Headman
The Doomsday Gang
Run for Your Life
The Terrible Love Life of Dudley Cornflower
Dracula, Go Home
The Ape Inside Me
Flames Going Out
The Ghost of Hellsfire Street
Brogg's Brain
Frank and Stein and Me
Crocker

Adult Titles

A Pride of Women
The Pushbutton Butterfly
The Kissing Gourami
Matchpoint for Murder
The Body Beautiful Murder
The Princess Stakes Murder
Dead as They Come
The Giant Kill
The Screwball King Murder
Murder in Rosslare